IN FOCUS...

SHARK HABITATS

Camilla de la Bédoyère

Quarto Library

This library edition published in 2020
by Quarto Library,
an imprint of The Quarto Group.
26391 Crown Valley Parkway,
Suite 220
Mission Viejo, CA 92691, USA
T: +1 949 380 7510
F: +1 949 380 7575
www.QuartoKnows.com

Distributed in the United States and Canada by
Lerner Publisher Services
241 First Avenue North
Minneapolis, MN 55401 U.S.A.
www.lernerbooks.com

A CIP record for this book is available from the Library of Congress.

ISBN: 978 0 7112 5541 8

Manufactured in Guangdong, China CC042020

9 8 7 6 5 4 3 2 1

MIX
Paper from responsible sources
FSC® C008047

CONTENTS

Words in **bold** are explained in the Glossary on page 31.

WHERE DO SHARKS LIVE?

Sharks live in all the oceans of the world, apart from the coldest waters of the Antarctic. Some sharks spend most of their lives in one area. Others, however, travel long distances in search of food, or to breed. These journeys are called **migrations**. Female blue sharks are known to travel an incredible 4,250 miles (6,840 kilometers) in a single migration.

Blue sharks are found in very deep waters.

The sixgill shark lives in deep water.

Habitats

Some sharks stay in the same region for their whole lives, and others swim from ocean to ocean. The type of place an animal lives is called its **habitat.** For many sharks, the habitat is the open ocean, far from land. Others prefer a coastal habitat, with shallow waters that are close to shore.

BITE-SIZE FACT

The bull shark can swim up large rivers, such as the Amazon, and can be found hundreds of miles from the sea.

Sharks are frequently seen in the red areas on this map.

Following the Food

Sharks live wherever they can find food. They are **adapted** to suit the habitat where they live. That is why sharks that live in open oceans and hunt **shoals** of small fish are fast swimmers. Sharks that live on the seabed are often slow swimmers.

Many sharks, such as sandbar sharks, live in shallow coastal water, where there is plenty of food.

SHARK HABITATS

Let's take a look at some of the habitats where sharks can be found.

Reef sharks swim through the reef, where they find plenty of fish to eat.

Coral Reefs

Coral reefs grow in warm, clean water near coasts. They are built by tiny animals called polyps and, over time, grow into huge rocky habitats where billions of creatures live. Sharks can find plenty of food at a coral reef, so it makes a good home.

In the Shallows

The sunlit, shallow waters close to coasts are perfect places for plants, such as mangroves, and seaweed to grow. They are a good place for sharks to hide their eggs. When the eggs hatch, the little pups stay in the shallow water, lurking in the shadows where bigger **predators** cannot find them.

A shark's egg is safe in its case.

Seasonal Homes

The chilly waters around the North and South Poles can be challenging for animals, but at certain times of year the cold oceans are full of life. In spring, thresher sharks swim to the cool waters of the North Atlantic Ocean to hunt huge shoals of mackerel. When winter comes, they migrate south to the warm waters of the tropics.

Camouflaged skin helps this shark to lurk, unseen, on the seabed.

BITE-SIZE FACT

Many **species** of shark live near the coast. Tiger sharks and bull sharks can swim in just a few feet of water.

Safe on the Sea Floor

Sharks that live in the open ocean are often large, **streamlined,** and colored gray and white. The sharks that live on the seabed are usually smaller, flatter, and **camouflaged** with patterned skin. Dark colors and patterns help them to hide as they lie in wait for unsuspecting animals to pass by.

CARPET SHARKS

Carpet sharks are usually found on the ocean floor, and are often colorful or patterned—just like a carpet! This clever disguise helps them to stay camouflaged.

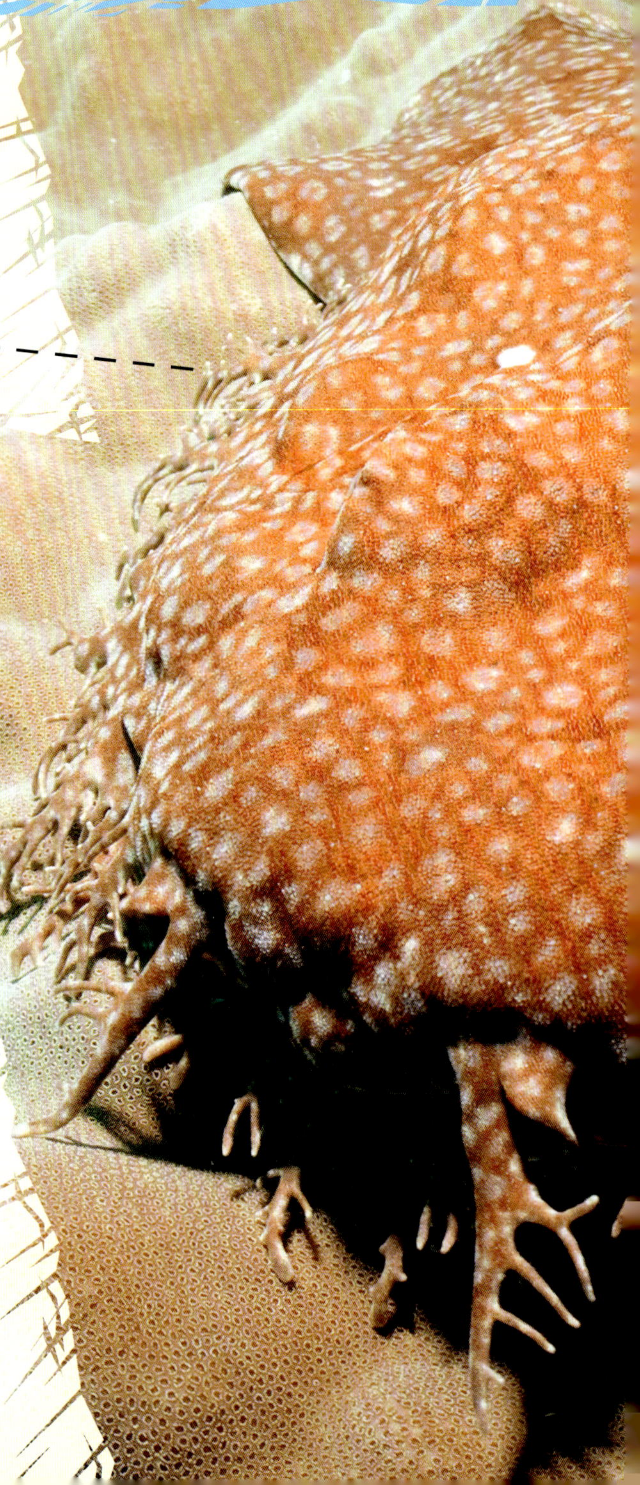

A tasseled wobbegong.

Barbels of a carpet shark.

Special Senses

There are about 42 types of carpet shark. They have a pair of sensitive feelers, called barbels, around their mouths that help them sense objects on the seabed.

Types of Carpet Shark

This large and varied group contains seven families of shark: collared carpet sharks, blind sharks, longtailed carpet sharks, wobbegongs, nurse sharks, the zebra shark, and the whale shark.

Most carpet sharks hunt animals that live on, or near, the seafloor.

BITE-SIZE FACT

Some carpet sharks can use their **pectoral fins** like limbs to "walk" along the seabed.

Sit and Wait

Most carpet sharks are slow swimmers. They either sit and wait for their prey, or creep up on them. However, they turn up the speed when they need to lunge forward and catch prey.

ANGELSHARKS

Angelsharks have broad, flat bodies. They look more like **rays** or **skates** than sharks, with blunt snouts and wing-like fins. They usually live near the seabed, where they bury their bodies beneath sand and mud, and wait for prey to pass.

Angelsharks are camouflaged on the seabed.

Monkfish

Angelsharks are sometimes also called monkfish. They are strong swimmers, but only swim in short spurts. Angelsharks often hunt at night and have tough teeth for grinding up the shells of sea creatures such as crabs and whelks.

Endangered

Most angelsharks live in coastal areas of the Atlantic and Pacific Oceans. They were once common, but now half of all angelshark species are on a list of **endangered** animals because they are fished for food and their skin is used to make leather. (Leather made from shark, ray, or skate skin is called shagreen.)

Angelsharks have two dorsal fins. Their gill slits are on the underside of their body.

BITE-SIZE FACT

The pectoral fins of an angelshark are very large, and look like wings. That is why they are named after angels.

Angelsharks bury themselves in sand. This one is almost invisible!

Bottom Dwellers

There are about 20 species of angelsharks. They are often patterned on their **dorsal** sides, so they blend in with the seabed, and pale underneath. They live in the northeast Atlantic and Mediterranean Sea, near the coast.

PORT JACKSON SHARK

Like other members of the bullhead shark family, a Port Jackson shark is perfectly suited to a life hunting on the seabed. Its patterned skin helps it stay hidden and the dark bands on its body even **mimic** shadows cast by sunlight passing through the sea.

BITE-SIZE FACT

Port Jackson sharks have sharp spines at the front of their dorsal fins.

Night Hunters

Port Jackson sharks hunt at night. They lie in wait for animals, such as starfish or octopuses, to pass by, or they swim close to the seabed, searching for prey. These sharks mostly use their sense of smell to find food.

Home Range

These sharks live along the coasts of Australia (except northern coasts) and nearby islands. Although they are not fished, they are often trapped in nets that have been put out to catch other fish.

This shark is unusual because its big, round **nostrils** are connected to its mouth.

On the Move

Bullhead sharks such as the Port Jackson don't just swim, they also use their fins to crawl along a rocky seabed. In the summer, they migrate closer to the shore where they lay their eggs.

The shark's pectoral fins are large and strong.

LEMON SHARK

Lemon sharks are large coastal sharks of the Pacific and Atlantic Oceans. They prefer to live in warm, shallow waters near land, especially during the day. At night they swim to deeper water and they can also rest on the seabed.

A lemon shark has a wide, flat head.

Lemon sharks get their name from the yellow-brown color of their skin.

Staying Safe

Pups are born between April and September. Each female can give birth to up to 17 pups at a time. They stay in their nursery areas for several years, where they are safe from adult lemon sharks, which sometimes eat them.

A remora fish attached to a lemon shark.

Sharksuckers

Remoras, or sharksuckers, are long, thin fish with a sucker on the top of their head. They use this to stick to a shark or other large fish and hitch a ride. Remoras feed off any scraps that the shark does not eat and also help sharks to stay healthy by eating their **parasites**. Some lemon sharks have been known to eat remoras.

BITE-SIZE FACT

Lemon sharks sometimes swim up rivers. They can adapt to different levels of salt concentration.

Magnetic Sensors

Lemon sharks have small eyes and poor eyesight. The coastal waters where they live are often cloudy, so eyesight is not a great help in finding prey. Instead, these fish have special magnetic **sensors** in their snout, which help them find fish and shelled animals on the seabed.

BLACKTIP REEF SHARK

Coral reefs provide a good habitat for many ground sharks, including blacktip reef sharks. The reefs are home to plenty of small animals for the sharks to hunt, including **invertebrates** and shoals of fish.

These reef sharks often gather in groups near the shore.

Energetic Hunters

Blacktip reef sharks live in warm, shallow waters. They are very good hunters and sometimes use a special technique in which they leap out of the water and rotate up to four times before splashing back in. They eat fish, squid, and crustaceans.

This shark's dorsal fins have black tips.

Peaceful Creatures

Blacktip reef sharks are often seen near the coast, but they usually swim away quickly if they are disturbed. They live in the warm waters of the southern Pacific Ocean, the Indian Ocean, and the eastern Mediterranean Sea.

BITE-SIZE FACT

This shark can swim in water that is just 12 inches (30 centimeters) deep!

A diver gets close to a reef shark.

Tourism

Divers enjoy watching blacktip reef sharks swimming around coral reefs, but these precious habitats are being damaged by **climate change** and **pollution.** As a result, the number of all reef sharks is expected to fall.

ZEBRA SHARK

Zebra sharks live in the Indian and south Pacific Oceans, in warm water and close to shore, although pups often stay in deeper water. Zebra sharks are often found around coral reefs. They lay their eggs on the seabed, then attach the eggs with tufts of hair.

Most zebra sharks grow to about 6.5 feet (2 meters) long.

Young sharks are called pups. This pup still has its stripes.

Spots and Stripes

When zebra sharks are young, they have stripes. When they get older, they have spots.

BITE-SIZE FACT

Zebra sharks suck little animals out of the sand, where they are hiding.

Camouflage

A zebra shark's stripes or spots are a type of camouflage. Camouflage helps them hide among seaweed and in shallow water. As the pups grow, they swim out to the deep ocean, and some of their stripy markings fade away.

Finding Food

Zebra sharks wriggle inside rocky holes to find small fish and crabs to eat. They often lie on the seabed with their mouths open and facing the **current**. Zebra sharks have small, spiked teeth.

The holes above this shark's small mouth are nostrils.

DOGFISH SHARKS

Dogfish sharks have two dorsal fins, which sometimes have sharp spines on them. They live throughout the world's oceans, and some species live in icy seas farther north than any other type of shark.

A Portuguese shark

Dorsal fin of a dogish shark

Swimming Deep

Many dogfish sharks live near land, but others live in the deepest parts of the ocean. Portuguese sharks have been found at depths of nearly 3,000 feet (just over 900 meters), where few other animals can survive.

Varied Group

There are about 130 types of dogfish sharks. This large group includes little lantern sharks that are able to glow in the deep, dark sea, as well as large, slow-moving sleeper sharks, which can grow to 26 feet (8 meters) long.

Lantern shark

BITE-SIZE FACT

Lantern sharks are probably the smallest sharks in the world—they are often less than 12 inches (30 centimeters) long.

At Risk

Dogfish sharks were once very common, but they have been overfished, mostly for food, in more than 50 countries. They are slow-moving, which makes them easy to catch. They also have few pups at a time, which means that populations of dogfish sharks are slow to recover once they have fallen.

GREENLAND SHARK

Greenland sharks live in the freezing waters of the Arctic. Like many other animals that live in cold places, these giant sharks move slowly and live long lives, to the age of 100 or more.

BITE-SIZE FACT

Greenland sharks are the biggest fish in the Arctic Ocean.

Hunting and Scavenging

Greenland sharks hunt almost anything, from small squid to whales and seals. They have about 100 little teeth, which they use to seize their prey. They also **scavenge** and they have been found with the **carcasses** of large land animals, such as reindeer, in their guts.

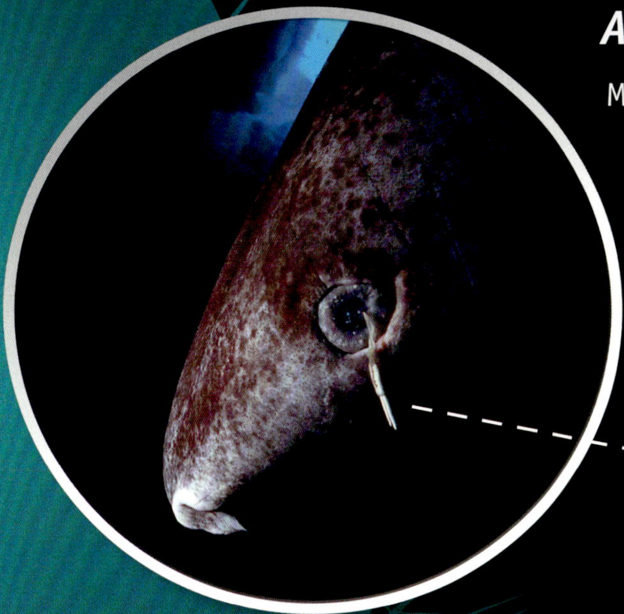

Almost Blind

Many Greenland sharks have copepods—small sea animals—attached to the front of their eyeballs. The copepods eat the transparent skin there and can make the sharks blind. This may be one reason why Greenland sharks sometimes scavenge instead of hunt.

A Greenland shark with a copepod parasite on its eye.

Toxic Shark

Greenland sharks can survive in icy Arctic waters because a chemical in their flesh works like an anti-freeze. This chemical also turns their flesh **toxic**, so it is poisonous to humans if it is eaten.

Although these sharks usually swim slowly, they can move with great bursts of speed when they hunt.

GOBLIN SHARK

Goblin sharks are mysterious fish that hunt in the deep oceans. They are slow swimmers that search for small fish in the dark. Scientists know very little about these sharks because very few have ever been found.

The jaw can move forwards to grab fish.

Different Teeth

The shark's teeth at the front of its jaws are very long and dagger-like. That is the perfect shape for grabbing small, slender fish. The teeth at the back of its jaws are the right shape for grinding up bones or shellfish.

BITE-SIZE FACT

A goblin shark skeleton is valuable because it is rare. Collectors will pay a lot of money to own one.

Lifecycle

No one knows where these sharks breed, or how many pups they have at a time. Goblin sharks can grow longer than 12 feet (3.6 meters), and they may live long lives as they probably have no predators.

Hunting

The strange snout may be part of the shark's **electro-sense**. It may be used to detect the movement of any other animals nearby—that is a useful skill for an animal that lives in the pitch dark.

FRILLED SHARK

Frilled sharks are mostly found near Japan, New Zealand, and in the eastern Atlantic Ocean. They prefer deep water, from 65 to 5,000 feet (20 to 1,525 meters), and are benthic fish. This means they live on or near the seabed.

The frilled shark is found in scattered patches across a wide range of ocean.

Rare shark

Frilled sharks are so rare, there are only two species that have been discovered so far. They are 3–6 feet (about 1–2 meters) long and have needle-sharp teeth, a broad mouth, and a short snout. They are sometimes called eel sharks because of their long, slender body shape and long tail fin.

Dagger-Like Teeth

Frilled sharks usually swim with their large mouths open, exposing rows of large teeth. Each tooth has three long, dagger-like points, called cusps. Frilled sharks are predators of deep-sea squid and bony fish.

Frilled sharks have 25 rows of razor sharp teeth.

Frilled sharks are named for their 12 frilly gill slits (six on each side of the head).

BITE-SIZE FACT

There are only two species of frilled shark: the frilled shark and the Southern African frilled shark.

Lifestyle

Like most other sharks, frilled sharks live alone. However, they travel inshore to mate in spring. Female frilled sharks give birth to about 10 pups at a time, and each one is about 16 inches (40 centimeters) long. Scientists think that these unusual sharks live for 50 years or more.

BLUE SHARK

These are the most graceful of all sharks. Blue sharks live in the open ocean, and they are one of the world's most widespread sharks. They can survive in all the world's oceans, including the warmest edges of the Arctic and Southern Oceans.

Blue sharks have a long, slender snout and large eyes.

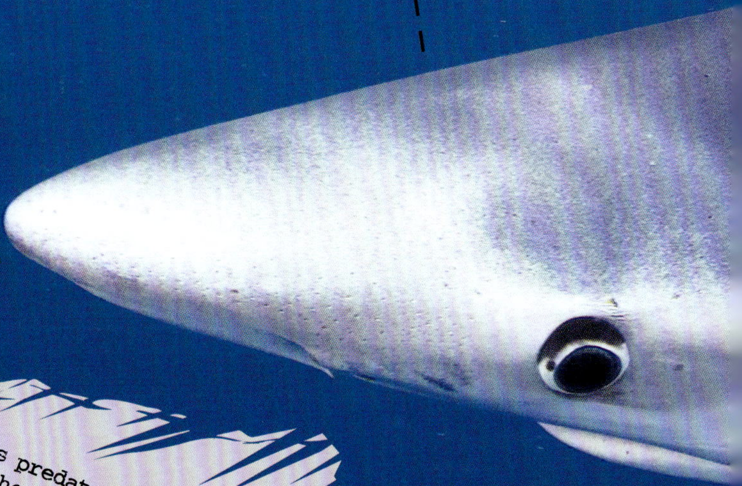

This predator feeds on shoals of fish, such as anchovies.

Long Distances

Blue sharks go on long journeys, called migrations. They can travel thousands of miles across the ocean because their bodies are a streamlined shape. The longest recorded migration for any blue shark is a journey of 3,740 miles (about 6,000 kilometers) from the coasts of New York to Brazil.

BITE-SIZE FACT

Many blue sharks are killed each year due to overfishing.

Filter Feeders

Although blue sharks are predators of fish and squid, they are also able to filter feed, like the whale shark, because their **gills** can trap small animals such as shrimp. Blue sharks also scavenge on big animals such as whales.

Life Cycle

Female blue sharks of the Atlantic Ocean mate in the western Atlantic before swimming across the seas toward European waters, following the ocean currents. They give birth in the eastern Atlantic and have 30 to 50 pups at a time.

CREDITS

Key: FC = front cover, BC = back cover, t = top, b = bottom, c = center, r = right, l = left.

Alamy:
8-9 WaterFrame; 18bl dpa picture alliance; 22-23 WaterFrame, 23tr louise murray.

Dreamstime:
8cl Ian Scott; 10bl Chris Moncrieff; 13br Irko Van Der Heide; 17br Irko Van Der Heide.

FLPA:
1 Bruno Guenard/Biosphoto; 10-11 Gerard Soury/Biosphoto, 11cl Flip Nicklin/Minden Pictures; 12-13 Fred Bavendam/Minden Pictures, 13tl Jeffrey Rotman/Biosphoto; 15tl Reinhard Dirscherl; 18-19 Fred Bavendam/Minden Pictures, 19bc Bruno Guenard/Biosphoto; 20br D P Wilson, 20-21 Kelvin Aitken/Biosphoto; 26-27 Kelvin Aitken/Biosphoto, 27tr Kelvin Aitken/Biosphoto; 32 Kelvin Aitken/Biosphoto.

Nature Picture Library:
6br Nature Production, 6-7 Fred Bavendam, 7c Pascal Kobeh; 9tr Richard Robinson; 21tr Florian Graner; 22cl Doug Perrine; 28-29 Chris & Monique Fallows.

SeaPics.com:
24bl David Shen, 24-25 e-Photo/Makoto Hirose, 25br e-Photo/Makoto Hirose.

Shutterstock:
FC frantisekhojdysz and Jolanta Wojcicka; BC Willyam Bradberry; 2 Ian Scott; 4bl Greg Amptman, 4-5 marina durante, 5bc Attila JANDI; 14cl nicolas.volsin44, 14-15 Dray van Beeck; 16bl Stybe Reineck, 16-17 Ian Scott; 26tr www.3drenderedlogos.com; 28cl Dray van Beeck, 29tl Greg Amptman; 30b Ian Scott.

The publisher gratefully acknowledges the permission granted to reproduce the copyright material in this book. Every effort has been made to trace copyright holders and to obtain their permission for the use of copyright material. The publisher apologizes for any errors or omissions in the above list and would be grateful if notified of any corrections that should be incorporated in future reprints or editions of this book.

GLOSSARY

adapt
how an animal changes to suit its home and lifestyle

camouflage
an animal's coloring that blends into the background

carcass
the dead body of an animal

climate change
the way that the Earth's climate changes over time. Most climate change is natural, but today humans are making the planet warmer and this is changing the climate

current
a flow of water through the ocean

dorsal
the back or upper surface of an animal's body

electro-sense
a sense that allows sharks to detect the electricity made in other animals' bodies

endangered
at risk of going extinct, or dying out forever

gill
a part of a fish's body that takes oxygen out of the water so the fish can breathe

habitat
an animal's natural home

invertebrate
an animal without bones

migration
a long journey in search of food, places to mate, or a new habitat

mimic
to copy or imitate another animal

nostril
the holes that lead into a nose or snout

parasite
an animal that feeds on another living animal and does it harm

pectoral fins
a pair of fins on either side of a fish's body, behind its head

pollution
a substance that damages the environment

predator
an animal that hunts and kills other animals to eat

ray
a flat fish in the same family of fish as sharks and skates

scavenge
to find dead animals to eat

sensor
part of the body that can be used to sense

shoal
a group of fish

skate
a flat fish in the same family of fish as sharks and rays

species
a type of animal or plant. Animals from the same species mate with each other and have young

streamlined
a body shape that is smooth and slim so the animal can move easily through water or air

toxic
poisonous

INDEX